Children
of the Earth... *Remember*

by Schim Schimmel

For my beautiful daughter, Sierra Mariah Schimmel.
Your life makes all the difference.

NORTHWORD PRESS
Chanhassen, Minnesota

Somewhere

in the deepest black velvet of space
there spins a brilliant blue world.

From afar
this world looks like a beautiful blue and white clouded marble.

But the closer
we get
the more
colors
we see —
reds and
browns
and yellows
and all shades
of green.

There are many worlds
spinning through space
but this world is special.

This is no ordinary world.

There are animals on this world.
Billions of animals.
More animals than all the
twinkling stars in the night sky.

And all of these animals are the children of this world.
For this world is their mother.

And we call this world
Mother Earth.

The animals are not alone on Mother Earth.
There are people living there, too.
Billions of people.
More people than all the twinkling stars in the night sky.
And all of these people are the children of Mother Earth, too.
So the animals and the people and Mother Earth
are all one big family.

And the dolphins play.

And the birds sing.

And the deer dance.

And the people live.

In the deepest black velvet of space
spins the family of Mother Earth.

And the animals remember.

They remember
Mother Earth
before there were people.

They remember how all the forests
were thick and lush and green.
How all the oceans and rivers and lakes
were pure and crystal clear.
How the sky was such a bright brilliant blue.

And the animals remember when they saw the first people.
In the beginning, very few.
But soon, more and more and more
until there were people everywhere on Mother Earth.

Still, there were more animals than people.
And the people shared Mother Earth with the animals.
They remembered that the animals
were their sisters and brothers.
They remembered that they were all part of one big family.

And the animals
and the people
were the eyes
and ears
and heart of
Mother Earth.

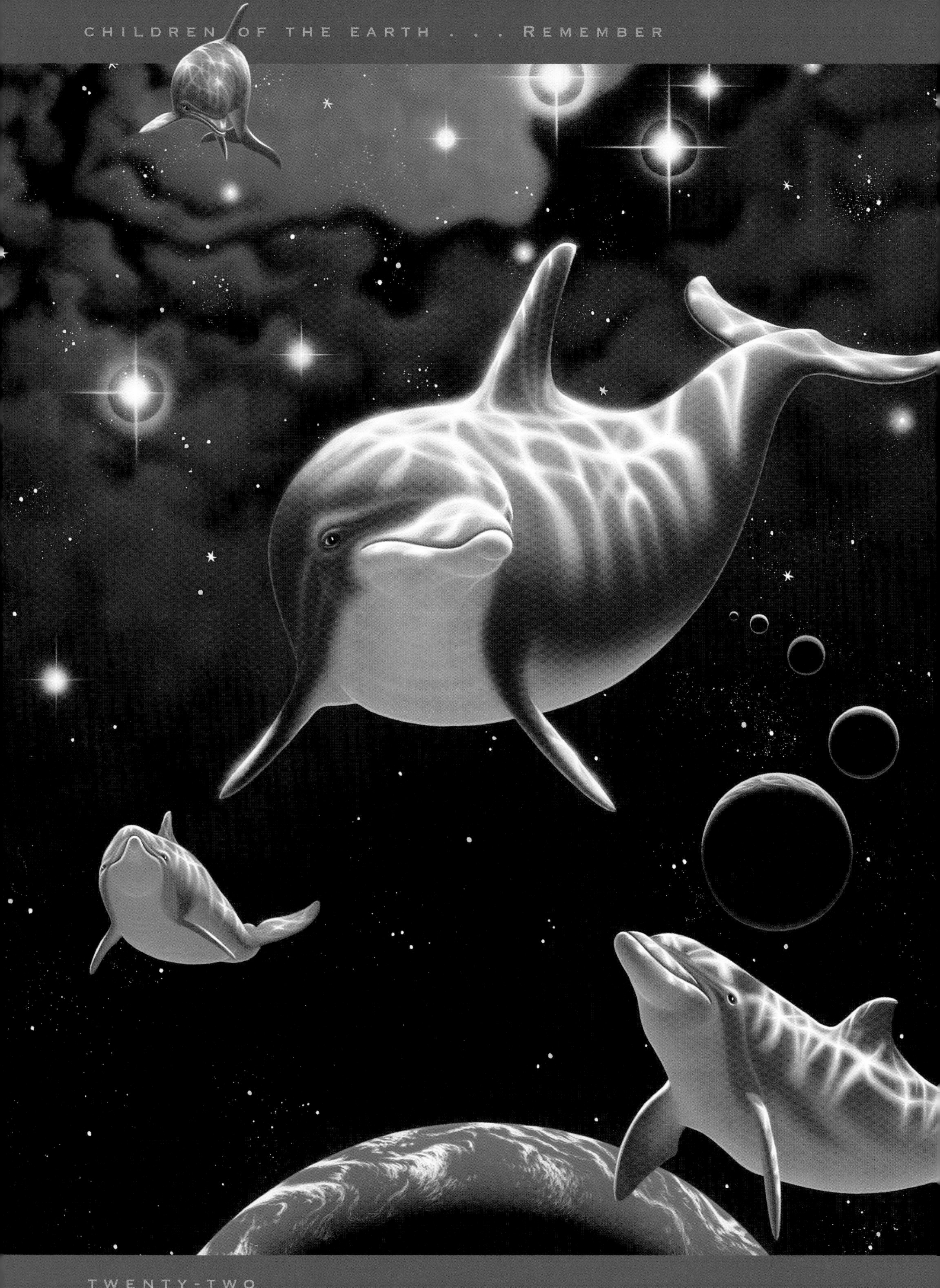

So when dolphins played
Mother Earth played.

When birds sang
Mother Earth sang.

When deer danced
Mother Earth danced.

And when people loved
Mother Earth loved.

Time passed and more people were born.
More and more and more people
until, finally, there were more people than animals.

And the
people
forgot.

They forgot to share
Mother Earth's land
and water and sky
with the animals.

They forgot that the animals were their sisters and brothers. They forgot that they were all part of the one big family of Mother Earth.

The people forgot.

But the animals remembered.
And they knew they would have to remind the people.
So every day our sisters and brothers remind us . . .

And when dolphins play
people remember.

When birds sing
people remember.

When deer dance
people remember.

And when people remember
they love.

Children
of the Earth . . . *Remember*
Schim Schimmel

Schim Schimmel describes his acrylic paintings as Environmental Visionary Surrealism. His message is that we must share this planet with all its varied life. "The central theme of my artwork and writing is the concept of planetary interdependency. I believe in an inherent unity and oneness pervading all manifested creation." Schim's artwork has been reproduced in prints, posters, puzzles, and other products throughout the world. This is his second children's book.

For more information on Schim's artwork, please call Collectors Editions/Art Impressions at 1-800-736-0001.

Cover and book design by Russell S. Kuepper and Schim Schimmel

NorthWord Press
18705 Lake Drive East
Chanhassen, MN 55317
1-800-328-3895

Library of Congress Cataloging-in-Publication Data
Schimmel, Schim
    Children of the Earth . . . Remember / by Schim Schimmel.
        p.   cm.
    Summary: Out of love and concern for their planet, the animals and people of Mother Earth work together to protect the natural world.
      ISBN 1-55971-640-1
      [1. Environmental protection--Fiction.] I. Title.
    PZ7.S346325Rj   1997
    [E]--dc21   97-9617
                         CIP

Printed in Singapore
10 9 8 7